For Dusty

Scholastic Canada Ltd.
604 King Street West, Toronto, Ontario M5V 1E1, Canada

Scholastic Inc.
557 Broadway, New York, NY 10012, USA

Scholastic Australia Pty Limited
PO Box 579, Gosford, NSW 2250, Australia

Scholastic New Zealand Limited
Private Bag 94407, Botany, Manukau 2163, New Zealand

Scholastic Children's Books
Euston House, 24 Eversholt Street, London NW1 1DB, UK

www.scholastic.ca

Nick used acrylic paint on paper to create these illustrations.
Typeset in Geist Serifa.

Library and Archives Canada Cataloguing in Publication
Bland, Nick, 1973-, author, illustrator
The very brave bear / by Nick Bland.
ISBN 978-1-4431-2841-4 (bound).
--ISBN 978-1-4431-2842-1 (pbk.)
I. Title.

PZ10.3.B527Veb 2014   j823'.92   C2013-903806-X

First published in Australia by Scholastic Australia Pty Limited.
This edition published in Canada by Scholastic Canada Ltd.

Text and illustrations copyright © 2014 by Nick Bland.

8 7 6 5 4 3   Printed in Malaysia 108   17 18 19 20 21

In the Jingle Jangle Jungle
on the edge of Slimy Bog,
Bear was picking berries
from a very wobbly log.

"AHOY!" said Boris Buffalo, from underneath the mud,
and Bear fell off his wobbly log and landed with a . . .

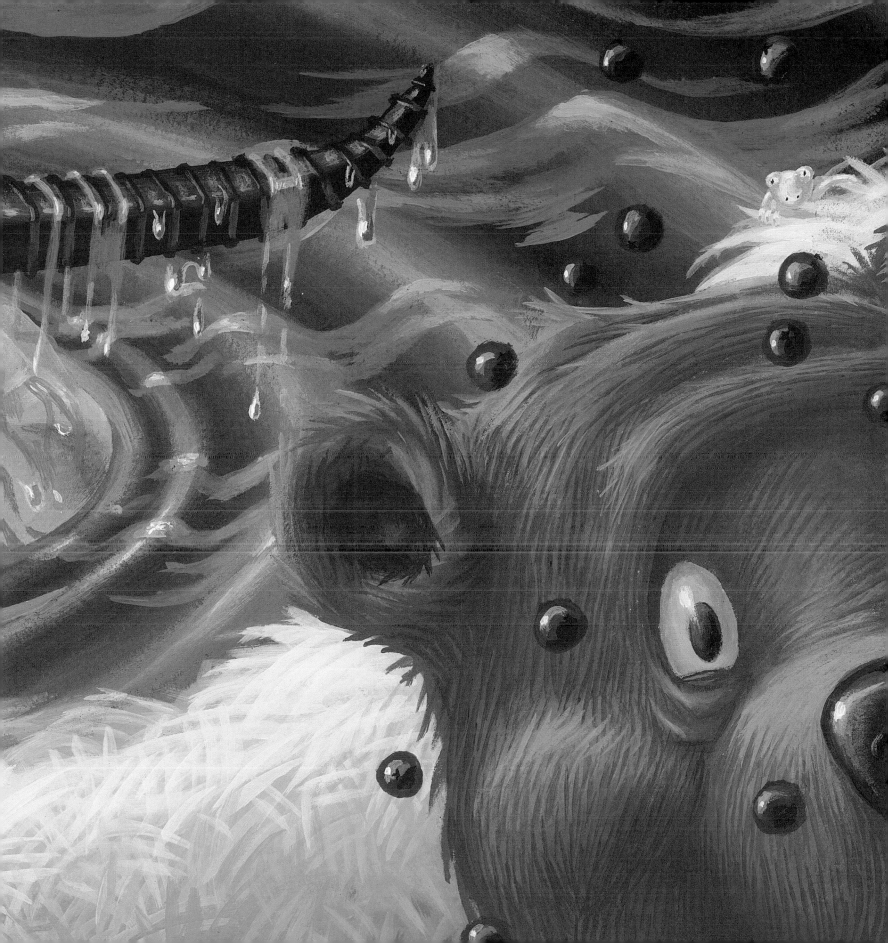

THUD.

"I didn't mean to **SCARE** you," said Boris with a grin. "I only came to ask you if you wanted to come in."

"I wasn't even scared," said Bear.
"I'm just as brave as you.
The **BRAVEST** thing that you can do,
I can do it, too."

So he balanced like a butterfly
upon the wobbly log.
He did a double somersault . . .

and **SPLASHED**
in Slimy Bog.

"If you're so brave," continued Bear, "then come and follow me. We'll see how brave a buffalo is when climbing up a tree."

So Bear climbed up a mighty tree,
the **TALLEST** he could find,
and there was Boris Buffalo,
climbing right behind.

"That was easy!" Boris said.
"And what a pleasant view.
But I can think of something else
that you'd be scared to do."

Boris wandered up a hill,
the **STEEPEST** he could find,

then tumbled down the other side

. . . and Bear was right behind.

They crossed a **RAGING** river,

and they **SWUNG** between the trees.

They tried to catch a **PORCUPINE**,

and wear a beard of **BEES**.

Bear and Boris Buffalo were the bravest of the brave,
until, that is, they came across . . .

A VERY SCARY CAVE!

"It's awfully dark inside," said Boris.
"It's quiet too," said Bear.
Then in his softest voice he said,
"Is anybody there?"

"Maybe we should wait," said Boris,
"until we know for sure."

And then, from in
the cave, there came
a very scary . . .

"ROAAAAR!"

Bear and Boris Buffalo had never been so **SCARED!**
They decided **NOT** to go inside, neither of them **DARED!**

They **HURRIED**
through the jungle,
and they **HID** in
Slimy Bog.

And then, from in the
cave, there came . . .

. . . a tiny little frog.

"I didn't mean to **SCARE** you," said Froggy with a grin.
"I only came to ask you if you wanted to come in."

So Bear and Boris Buffalo went back to Froggy's cave,
and agreed that bears and buffaloes . . .

. . . are equally as brave.